Grounded

George Brant

D0071518

A SAMUEL FRENCH ACTING EDITION

FOUNDED 1830

SAMUELFRENCH.COM
SAMUELFRENCH-LONDON.CO.UK

FOR PRODUCTION ENQUIRIES

UNITED STATES AND CANADA
Info@SamuelFrench.com
1-866-598-8449

UNITED KINGDOM AND EUROPE
Plays@SamuelFrench-London.co.uk
020-7255-4302

Each title is subject to availability from Samuel French, depending upon country of performance. Please be aware that *GROUNDED* may not be licensed by Samuel French in your territory. Professional and amateur producers should contact the nearest Samuel French office or licensing partner to verify availability.

MUSIC USE NOTE

Licensees are solely responsible for obtaining formal written permission from copyright owners to use copyrighted music in the performance of this play and are strongly cautioned to do so. If no such permission is obtained by the licensee, then the licensee must use only original music that the licensee owns and controls. Licensees are solely responsible and liable for all music clearances and shall indemnify the copyright owners of the play(s) and their licensing agent, Samuel French, against any costs, expenses, losses and liabilities arising from the use of music by licensees. Please contact the appropriate music licensing authority in your territory for the rights to any incidental music.

IMPORTANT BILLING AND CREDIT REQUIREMENTS

If you have obtained performance rights to this title, please refer to your licensing agreement for important billing and credit requirements.

The New York premiere of *GROUNDED* was presented by Page 73 Productions, Liz Jones and Asher Richelli, Executive Directors; Michael Walkup, Producing Director, at Walkerspace at Soho Rep. The opening date was January 16, 2014 The performance was directed by Ken Rus Schmoll, with sets and costumes by Arnulfo Maldonado, lighting by Garin Marschall, and sound by Jane Shaw. The Production Stage Manager was Megan Schwarz Dickert. The cast was as follows:

THE PILOT . . . . Hannah Cabell

GROUNDED was first produced in a rolling World Premiere by SF Playhouse (California), Borderlands Theater (Arizona), and Unicorn Theatre (Missouri) as part of the National New Play Network's Continued Life program.

CAST

THE PILOT – a woman in her mid-to-late 30's. She should have no allergies or asthma after 12 years of age, distant vision of at least 20/200 but corrected to 20/20, and near vision of 20/40 but corrected to 20/20. She should have a sitting height of between 2 foot 9 inches and 3 foot 4 inches, and a vertical standing height of between 5 foot 4 inches and 6 foot 5 inches tall. She should possess normal color vision and meet other physical weight requirements, with no more than 32% body fat. She should be able to complete a 1.5 milerun in 13 minutes and 56 seconds or less, as well as complete 50 sit-ups and 27 push-ups in a timed test of one minute each. She should have graduated at the top of her class and have a well-rounded education. She should possess heightened situational awareness.

DESIGN

The sound and lighting design will play an important role in the production, reinforcing The Pilot's mental landscape and contributing a growing sense of unease throughout. The design should be more abstract than literal, or perhaps transform the literal into abstract.

Productions are invited to create their own melody for "The Pony Song."

PERFORMANCE

The telling of this story must be active, allowing for a full range of emotion; the end must not be played at the beginning.

The audience is The Pilot's confidante, to varying degrees of familiarity, until perhaps the final pages.

When other characters enter The Pilot's story, the Pilot does not fully inhabit them; she is not an actress.

SPECIAL THANKS

The author wishes to gratefully acknowledge the following organizations and
individuals who generously contributed to the development of *Grounded*:
(in order of appearance)

WordBRIDGE Playwrights Laboratory and Generous Company, Mike
Vandercook, Rebecca Eastman, David White, Erik Ramsey, Michele Minnick,
Theatre 4, Mariah Sage, Derek Goldman, Liz Frankel, Jessica Amato, National
New Play Network, Timothy Jay Smith, Jason Loewith, Jojo Ruf, Nan Barnett,
The Unicorn Theatre, Cynthia Levin, Vanessa Severo, Lieutenant Colonel
George J. Alston, Playwrights Foundation, Amy Mueller, Erin Merritt, Mollie
Stickney, Rebecca Henderson, Georgetown University, Kimberly Gilbert,
Michael Bloom, Manhattan Theatre Club, Mandy Greenfield, Jerry Patch,
Annie MacRae, Ana Reeder, The Gate Theatre, Christopher Haydon, Clare
Slater, Rachael Williams, Katy Munro-Farlie, Lucy Ellinson, Caroline Byrne,
The Traverse Theatre, Orla O'Loughlin, Emma Callander, San Francisco
Playhouse, Bill English, Lauren English, Susannah Martin, Jordan Puckett,
Borderlands Theatre, Barclay Goldsmith, Alida Holguin Gunn, Page 73, Liz
Jones, Asher Richelli, Michael Walkup, Ken Russ Schmoll, Hannah Cabell,
Carla Noack, City Theatre, Tracy Brigden, Jenn Thompson, Kelly McAndrew

With special thanks to
the New Harmony Project, Paul Walsh, Joel Grynheim
and
Maggie Lacey, Laura Epperson, Anna Rhoads,
Erica Nagel and Laura Kepley

For Laura

(Lights rise on **THE PILOT,** *a woman dressed in an Air Force flight suit.)*

THE PILOT.

    I never wanted to take it off
    Staring at myself in the mirror
    Myself in this
    I had earned this
    This was me now
    This was who I was now who I'd become through sweat
    and brains and guts
    This is me

    It's more than a suit
    It's the speed
    It's the G-Force pressing you back as you tear the sky
    It's the ride
    My Tiger
    My gal who cradles me lifts me up
    It's more
    It's the respect
    It's the danger
    It's
    It's more
    It's
    You are the blue
    You are alone in the vastness and you are the blue
    Astronauts
    They have eternity
    But I have color
    I have blue

    I'm in the blue for a reason
    I have missiles to launch

I have Sidewinders
I have Mavericks

I rain them down on the minarets and concrete below me
The structures that break up the sand
I break them back down
Return them to desert
To particles
Sand

At least I think I do
I'm long gone by the time the boom happens
Tiger and I are on to another piece of sky

Boom
Boom goes Saddam's dipshit army and then I'm home on leave
Wyoming
Leave is fine but it's slow
Slow and the blue is there everywhere but far away
Far

So I go to a bar
Pilot bar
I drink with my boys and we tell stories about flying
We try to make it into words
You can get close
But you never can

A guy comes up to me
A guy always comes up
No not always
It takes balls
Hard to casually sidle up to a bunch of drunk Air Force on leave
Maneuver yourself through all the boys to get to me
That takes some offensive flying of its own

But the guy makes it through

Gets up from a card game and runs the gauntlet to get
to me
He's kinda cute
I tell him straight off who I am what I am
I've learned not to wait
Once they find out
They tend to run away
Most guys don't like what I do
Feel they're less of a guy around me
I take the guy spot and they don't know where they
belong

But not this one
This one's eyes light up
This one thinks it's cool
This one kisses me in the parking lot like I'm the rock
star I am
He's not afraid to kiss me

Eric
He's Eric
I take him home
We fuck
First time's okay
Then he asks me to put my suit on
He says please
I tell him just once

Just telling him is enough
He's hard as a Sidewinder
It's a good three days
A very good three days

He tells me he can feel the sky in me
I tell him he's crazy
But something shifts
Something's breached

I'm back downrange

First time I'm sad leave is over
Shit
For Eric who works in a hardware store the family store
Shit
Like some 50's movie
I've got my little woman at home know who I'm
fighting for
All that true corn
True cheese

Lucky I got shit to distract me
I got tracer fire
I got RPGs
And I've got the blue
It's good to be back in the blue
Alone in the blue

Back at base I got webcams
I got Eric with a little delay
He misses me
I miss him too

I gain weight
Does love make you heavy?
I feel the harness tight against my waist
Try to watch the burgers in the caf
Hold the burgers
It's not the burgers

I'm up in the blue and I almost hurl in my mask
Make it down just in time to puke on the tarmac
Tell the boys I drank too much last night
Do a test
Pink
I'm pink
Pink
Fuck

I can't fly with it

With her
I know it's a her
I can't
Rules and regulations

It's the ejection seat
'Cause an ejection would be an ejection
A G-Force abortion

I want the sky
I want the blue
But I can't kill her
I can't kill her
I can't

I take one last flight
The both of us
So she can have a taste of what it means
Get it in her blood
Let her know that there is this
That this could be hers one day
That she will not be a hair-tosser
A cheerleader
A needy sack of shit
There is this
There is blue

And then I land
March to my Commander
I tell him
He's sorry-happy
I know the feeling

They run tests
Ultrasound
I see her
There in the grey
Looks like she's waving

I pack my suit

Say goodbye to Tiger
They ship me out
Stateside

They put me behind a desk
Grounded
The pilot's nightmare
Eric thinks I'm still in the desert still flying
His fantasy girl up in the sky

I don't know how to tell him what to tell him what I
want what he'll want
I decide it's worth finding out

I hide my belly under the desk
Skype him
Small talk then boom
There's a delay
That fucking delay
Then tears
I can feel them through the screen
He's so happy
And I didn't know it until then but I'm happy he's
happy
And we smile and I feel him here with me Eric's here
delay or not he's here months till I can see him for real
but he's here

More tests
They're a little worried about her
Stick a camera up me
Get a good look
She should be okay

My belly
My belly presses against the desk
Harder
Harder
Too big for the desk now

Air Force sends me on my way
The boys raise a glass
Hope I'll be back soon
Count on it assholes

Deep breath
I go to Eric's
White-knuckled the whole drive
Skype is one thing but
I can't hide my belly offscreen anymore
These fucking stretch marks
I'm not who left
I'm not who he
Shut up
I suck it up and ring the bell
Ready to see his face fall to see whatever flygirl fantasy
he's got going dispelled by the civilian whale before
him
He opens the door
He looks at me
He cries instead
He touches my belly
He kisses it and I feel things shift again
I smile
Am I crying now?
Fuck
He wants to take my picture
With my suit on
I tell him I can't fit anymore
He says, "I know. Please."
I say if we go outside
If the sky's in the background

I must look ridiculous
Can't zip up the front
Naked tight belly spilling out

(for the camera) Cheese
We go back inside
He puts it up on his computer
As his desktop
He says, "Demi Moore can kiss your ass."
And godammit he's right

We laugh
He stops laughing
He gets down on his knee
Shit
I pull him up
That's not how I want it
This is how I want it
And I throw him on his single bed
And I get on top
And we fuck
He fucks the whale
And I tell him I scream
Yes
Yes
Yes

Eric moves in
I say I do and he does too
The cheese I know the corn
It sneaks in
Love sneaks it in

Then we're three
I'm right
It's a girl
Samantha
Sam
A perfect girl

But not too perfect

She's got a spark in her eye
She's gonna be trouble
Like I said perfect

Maybe a little small
A little early
But that's okay
Just means we have to watch out for her at first

First

few

years

Keep an eye on her
Keeps me at home
Keeps me away from the blue
But that's fine
Every night Eric points to the sky and tells Sam "that's Mommy, that's where Mommy lives"
But she doesn't get it and it's not where I live anymore and so I tell him to stop

I love her and him I do I ignore the tight ball-bearing in my sternum I do for years three years but it grows it grows I'll scream if I don't get out and up I was born for this but I was born for that too I don't can't can't not be there be up alone alone in my sky

I don't know how to tell him
How to tell him I need more than this
That he is not everything
That she is not
She is he is but –
He stops me
He understands
He wants me to go
Excited even
Says he'll get his bragging rights back

I kiss him
This is why I married you this is why you are mine
We fuck and it is a fierce and wonderful thing

…

I report to my Commander
He's happy to see me
Was waiting for me
Tells me I'm needed now more than ever
Pilots pilots are the most needed
It's a new desert now Iraq is done stick a fork in it
I tell him fine different desert same war
I am ready to suit up
Tiger I want Tiger back she must have missed me she
will embrace me and lift me back up into the blue

Commander smiles a funny smile
He says, "New plane"

I say new plane?
But Tiger

The funny smile again
He says, "Forget Tiger. New plane, the newest."

Fuck
A new
I think of breaking it in
The seat the stick the pain in my ass but then I think
I do think
I'm sorry Tiger but I think
It's new
Brand new
It's the latest
I think of the speed
The firepower
That I will be the first to fly her
That she will be mine all mine

I think of all that and a smile sneaks out
I nod and say can I see her?

That funny smile again
He pulls a picture out of a folder

I think it's a joke

I say this is a drone

"No," he says, "it's a Reaper"

I say it's a drone

He says, "It's the newest we have, the best we have"

I say this is a drone
You want me in the Chair Force

He tells me careful, that is not its name that I know
better that that is not its name

I say you want to stick me in the Chair Force
I am a real pilot a fighter pilot I can help let me help

He says, "This is how you help
This is what we need
This is the war"

I say bullshit
A million dollars to train me
You don't spend a million dollars so I can fly a remote
control plane
You need fighter pilots
You always need fighter pilots
I say is this punishment?

He says, "What?"

I say for getting pregnant is this how you punish me?

He says, "No, no," he says, "listen. You'll be hunting
down the real bad guys, conducting personality strikes"

I say sir –

He says, "Just try it for a few months, and we'll
see –"

I say sir no one ever comes back from the Chair Force
it's the Bermuda Triangle no one ever comes back

He says, "I realize it's an adjustment"

I say sir with all due respect –

He says, "Major? Shut the fuck up."
He says, "I know how it is
I know all you F-16s love being worshipped I know you
love being top shit
I know
So listen to me
Carefully
I am not asking you to give that up
Because top shit will come top shit is on its way
There was a time the bomber pilot was top shit you're
too young you wouldn't remember
It's use
Use
Which one is useful
Which one gets the job done
They're not making F-16s anymore Major
The F-16s are dinosaurs
Put out to pasture
Used for drone target practice
The drones?
Can't make 'em fast enough
Five years, tops
Two
Fuck one
In one year
The drone will be king
And you
Patience
You will be top shit again
Dismissed"

.

I can't look Eric in the eye when I tell him
UAVs
Unmanned Aerial Vehicles
A drone pilot
A proud member of the Chair Force

He says, "When do you leave?"
I say when do we leave?
He says, "What?"
I say how do you feel about Vegas?
He says, "What?"

I say I will be in the war by way of Las Vegas
I will operate out of Creech Air Force base in Nevada
I will not live on the base there are no barracks on the
base
I will work seven days a week a twelve-hour shift and
then each night I will come home home to you and
Sam

Well?

The tears again
They are not weakness in him they are what I love
He says, "We'll be together the three of us we'll still be
together it's a gift a gift"

A gift
I will look at it that way I will try to look at it like that
A gift
The drones are a gift
I have been given a gift
I get to fly again
Sort of
But I will not be eight thousand miles away while I do it
I will see my daughter grow up
I will kiss my husband goodnight every night
No tracer fire

No RPGs
The threat of death has been removed
The threat of death has been removed from our lives
Viva
Viva
Viva Las Vegas

...

We get a small place in the suburbs
An anonymous home
Fill it with our things ourselves
Eric puts the picture on the wall the one of me with
the belly and the blue
He looks for a job
I watch Sam and unpack and count the hours till I
have to report
Until I become something else something less
Stop
We do the Strip a few times
It's bullshit
That fucking fake Pyramid
What the fuck
We see some bullshit shows
Neil Diamond
Some Beatles circus thing
Don't ask me
Fuck

And then it's time
0700 Eric kisses me goodbye I kiss Sam
I hop in my car and drive downrange

I have a fast car
Surprise
It takes me out of the driveway
Out of the suburbs into the desert
The Pyramid is behind me

Smaller smaller
The radio gets fuzzy goes static
The Pyramid disappears
And I am alone
Alone in the desert
An hour of quiet
Of static

The base rises out of the sand
Creech
Some name
Like a monster from a shitty movie

I'm downrange
Downrange after an hour's drive

I'm saluted
The gate rises
I find a space
A parking space
A pilot who needs a parking space
I put on my flight suit
A grounded pilot who wears a flight suit
I report for duty
For training
For retraining
For drones

First we stand sweating on the tarmac
Look at one in a crate
They're stored in pieces in crates
Excuse me Tombs
Tombs
The pieces are removed from the Tombs
Assembled on the tarmac
Like a toy model

We walk around a finished one

The last time we'll see one in person
Last time a pilot will see her plane
Ridiculous
A bunch of grounded pilots staring at a pilot-less plane
A plane with no cockpit
A bird with no eyes

The Reaper
11 million dollars
They tell us that bunch of times
11 million

It's bigger than I thought
Wings twice as wide as Tiger's
And loaded
Sidewinders
Stingers
Hellfires
Fucker's loaded

And turns out it's not blind after all
This camera system mounted on its belly:
The Gorgon Stare:
Infrared
Thermal
Radar
Laser
A thousand eyes staring at the ground

We go inside
We sit in a row at desks
Like we're in a typing class
Like we're learning how to make a spreadsheet
We learn to fly instead
We learn to fly with our asses firmly on the ground

It's bullshit
I pick it up quick
Not that that matters

Not that that's a source of pride

The only tricky part is the screen
The belly
You're not looking out you're looking down
Like you're in a cloud looking down
Take some getting used to

The rest
It's crazy
You move the joystick
1.2 seconds later the plane moves
1.2 seconds from anywhere in the world
You might as well be in the cockpit
You're not but you might as well

Oh and this:
They never land
Can stay up in the air for 40 hours at a time
We'll be working in shifts
Tapping each other out and taking the controls
A never-ending mission

I am dismissed
It's dark out now
I drive through the desert
Static becomes AC/DC
Thank you
The Pyramid gets closer
And I'm home

Eric asks how my day was
I am limited in my response
Like a teenager but with the justification of security
clearance
I say fine
My day was fine

Sam's already in bed

I kiss her perfect forehead goodnight and then eat the dinner my husband has prepared for me and we watch TV and go to sleep

Home will be training too
Getting used to the routine
Driving to war like it's shift work
Like I'm punching the clock
Used to transition home once a year
Now it'll be once a day
Different
Definitely different

But on the true corn hand
Knowing what you're fighting for and all that
I'll have a daily reminder
Not some dream Sam and Eric in my head half-remembered
But there
In front of me
Real
As real as a goodnight kiss

Rest of training's fine
A couple of the boys crash theirs
Oops
Be hard to work that off
Good thing they're not real yet
Not that we can tell the difference sitting in the typing pool

I don't crash mine
Not that it matters
But I don't

Sam misses me at dinnertimes begs to stay up till I get home
I tell her it's too late but we'll make mornings extra-special

I talk like a mom now
A bullshit one

Training over
I've earned a pin
The Chair Force pin
This lame-ass lightening bolt piece of shit
They stick it on my suit
Puncture my suit with the pin so it becomes part of it
part of me
I try not to look in the mirror

…

First day on the job
The war
Whatever
Eric makes me French toast for our extra-special
breakfast
He hands me my lunch in a brown paper bag and I'm
off to the desert to be a pilot
To be of use

I park in my spot and I put on my flight suit and enter
a trailer
One of many trailers in a parking lot
An air-conditioned trailer that seals me off completely
from all sky all blue

Fuck

My eyes adjust
I am guided to a Naugahyde Barcalounger
I tap the guy in it out
He gives me a nod
I sit
In front of me is a toy throttle and a screen
To the right of me is a 19 year-old chewing gum
He is the Sensor
He will control the cameras

The 19 year-old has been doing this a while
He is part of my team
I have a team now
A headset full of backseat drivers
Analysts advisers JAGs
My lone wolf days are over I don't call the shots anymore
I'm like the back-up singer for Neil Diamond

(Pause as she listens to "Sweet Caroline" in her head, waiting for her turn to sing:)

(singing) BUM-BUM-BUM

That's me
A team

I take the controls
I stare at the screen eighteen inches from my face
A Gorgon Stare
I stare at the desert
They're twelve hours ahead there
Night
Weird
I stare at the screen

It's not like a videogame
A videogame has color
I stare at grey
At a world carved out of putty
Like someone took the time to carve a putty world for me to stare at twelve hours a day
High definition putty

I'm told my mission for the day
To provide support for a convoy
A convoy on the screen in the real downrange
Look out for them
Make sure no bad guys're planting any IEDs
I am told to guide my plane over a road

I'm told to fly left
I fly left
Right
I fly right
Left right left right left

I'm told to orbit
To circle a spot on the ground
Stare at the sand from above
Staring down from above
That stupid song that song?
Seals and Crofts or Alan Parsons or somebody?
The eye in the sky
That's me
That's me now
I fly a plane and stare at a screen that stares at the
ground

I don't see anything
And that's good
Just grey putty
Nothing
Nothing
Nothing
Nothing
I'm tapped on the shoulder
A pilot takes my place takes control of my plane
Its not my plane anymore I don't have a plane anymore
It's his
He will stare at nothing now
And I
I will go home

I get in my car
My eyes adjust to color to the distance
Static
AC/DC again somebody up there likes me

I hold sleeping Sam against me
She is real and alive and warm
I eat dinner and I watch another screen and I go to
bed

Extra-special morning time and then I cross the desert
to look at a screen
Convoy
Nothing
Grey

Home
Eric tells me he's found a job at the Pyramid
Blackjack dealer
Cheating people out of money
I call him the Predator
We celebrate
I'm on top of him and I close my eyes and I see grey
for a second
Eric asks what's wrong I say nothing
I jerk him off and we watch the screen and call it a
night

The Pyramid is 24 hours too
Eric's the new guy gets the shit shift
The red-eye
Means I have to drop Sam off at day care now
An extra-special drop off
Kiss her goodbye and go to war
Sit in a car and cross the desert to sit in a chair in a
freezing trailer
To follow the convoy

Follow the convoy

The convoy

I'm jolted awake by laughter
I've fallen asleep and hit my head on the screen and
that is funny

A riot
Turns out they were taking bets how long it would take
Everybody does it they say
Sooner or later everybody –

Wait
I see something
A dot which zooms in to a man which pans to be several
men by the side of the road two miles up from our boys
They are doing something
They are doing something to the road
They are military age males
You can tell
The cameras are that good you can tell
You can tell how old if they're women men children
You can't see faces
Not really
But you don't need to your mind fills them in

And these are the faces of military age males by the
side of the road
I notify the team
Await confirmation
The headset pronounces the males guilty

I feel my pulse quicken
Ridiculous
I'm sweating my pits my hands
I'm not there I can't be killed the threat of death has
been removed there is no danger to me none I am the
eye in the sky there is no danger but my pulse quickens
why does it quicken
I am not in combat if combat is risk if combat is danger
if combat is combat I am not in it
But my pulse quickens
It is not a fair fight
But it quickens

I wait
The eye in the sky waits for the putty people to get
closer together
Just a little closer
Closer
Closer
There

I press the button
I watch the screen
A moment
A moment
And
boom
A silent grey boom

Oops
One of them is running a squirter one is still alive
My 19 year-old follows the squirter with the camera
I follow him with the plane
He is below us
I push the button
boom
He is not

We cheer
The team and I
I high-five my 19 year-old
The guilty are gone
I did this
We did this

We are thanked by the convoy
We say no problem
I'm vibrating
My knuckles are white white
Was I flying was that flying
They're white like they used to be

White

I go to the john
Piss
I sit there my hands shaking
I get a coffee
Get back in my chair
Look at the grey for another six hours
Searching for more of the guilty
Hoping to do it again

I'm tapped out
I want to celebrate
To grab a beer with the boys
But we're all on different shifts
Nobody stays here
So I don't stay here
I go home

"Your suit"
Eric says
"Why do you still have your suit on?"
I look down
It's on all right
I come up with something
I wanted to see you as soon as I could or something
He asks how my day was
I tell him fine but I tell him in a way that he knows it
was more than fine that I killed me some military age
males today
He smiles
We eat
We stare at a screen and then go to sleep

Drop Sam off
Drive through the desert
Stare at a screen at a road in a desert
A road that's twelve hours ahead

But only 1.2 seconds away

Oops
White-knuckle time
They're baaaack
Well not the same ones obviously but
Military age males by the side of the road
Headset gives a verdict a guilty a go
My 19 year-old locks the laser sights
Look at my fucking hands

And them
Look at them
Poor saps
You don't learn do you
You can't hide from the eye in the sky my children
We look down from above we see all and we have
pronounced you guilty
boom
Another grey inferno
A massive grey –

Are those?
I didn't notice that last time
Flying through the air
Body parts
Those must be body parts
Huh
Body parts

Guilty body parts

Static
AC/DC
Home
Eric is happy had a good day at the Pyramid
Getting the hang of it
Didn't lose too much for the Man
I ask him if he likes it

He says he does weird to be watched all the time but
he does
I say I bet you're watched
He says, "Not that,
Security, the eye"

Ah ,
Eric's got his own eye in the sky
The Pyramid watches him my husband
I tell him to be careful keep his nose clean
Don't want to end up like
He laughs
I ask to play him cards
He says c'mon
I insist
I don't win a game
My man's got some moves

Some stealthy ones too
He leaves the bedroom at 0200 to go to work without
me ever knowing
I sleep like the dead till my alarm goes off
Always wake surprised he's gone

Sam's suspicious
Wonders what makes a morning extra-special all I do
is drop her off
Smart kid

Back to the grey
It's funny
The screen isn't that big
But it becomes your world
Like the TV I guess
Or the computer
But the grey is

It definitely

In a dark trailer

Even grey

Jeep
There's a jeep
Who drives a jeep in the desert?
The guilty
The guilty do

It's not fair
Not really
We should make an announcement:
Attention People of the Grey Desert
Everything is Witnessed
The Moment You Step Outside You are Under Suspicion
That would be fair

Anyway
The jeep the grey jeep is driving too fast
Too fast to be innocent too fast for me to really see who's in it but the speed is guilt enough
My team confers
The headset gods of the sky
Was it Olympus?
Is that right?
Olympus debates the fate of the lowly jeep
Who knew?
Olympus is a trailer in the middle of the desert
We issue a judgement
I guide the plane
Give the jeep a little lead time
I press the button
boom
No more jeep

We sit and linger then

We do that a lot we drone–gods
Linger over what we've done
Orbit above and watch the grey flames dart

Our jeeps arrive on the scene
Same grey different jeeps
They inspect what we hath wrought
We linger for another hour or two and we move on to another piece of sky
Gaze down upon the guilty and the innocent both on all our children we watch over you my children we protect and destroy you yes Virginia there is a Santa Claus above you and there is a ninth reindeer and her name is Hellfire

Shift done
Out of the morning into the night
I keep my suit on again
Intentionally this time
Maybe that'll be our code Eric and me maybe that's how he'll know
Know if I've done good today if I have smote the enemy
"She has her suit on it was a good day"

AC/DC?
What the fuck

Eric sees the suit
He gets it
He gets it cause he's Eric
We celebrate
The screen and I'm falling asleep wrapped up in him and I realize the Commander was right we are the top shit we get to kick ass and screw our husbands and kiss our kids' forehead goodnight and that's something a fighter pilot never had never

I dream of it though
I dream of blue all the same

...

A month of grey
Of nothing
Of camera eye searching searching
Eric gives me a wink tells me nice work
I don't get it till I look down
The suit
I keep forgetting

I've earned leave
A week
Eric offers to take off too
Family vacation
No
I don't think so
Sam and I need our special time

First day of leave take her to the mall
It's too hot to walk around outside but I need to walk
to move I don't move enough anymore
Sam's moving
Hopping up and down so excited vibrating special
time special time
I look up
See the little black circle in the corner of the wall
They're watching us
Someone is watching us
That's fine
Fair enough
But Attention People of the Boulevard Mall:
My Daughter is Not the Guilty and her Stroller is Not
a Jeep
We Are the Innocent
You Let Us Pass

I go into a changing room
Take off my shirt

Look for the camera
Can't find it
But there's always a camera right
JC Penney or Afghanistan
Everything is Witnessed

I think of them
The 19 year–olds who surveille the dressing rooms
Or maybe they're not 19
Maybe you have to be older to watch naked people
Where's their room?
Their team?
Are they in the basement?
The parking lot?
They could be anywhere
Hell they could even be in India I guess
Another outsourced job
A great one
Watching fat Americans try on swimsuits

What if
What if these Indians watching us eventually come
here for a vacation but find themselves drawn to JC
Penney they don't know why but they are and when
they get there they go right past the sale racks right
past the shoes they head straight to the changing room
they don't know why they have nothing to change they
walk in they close the door and they suddenly know
why they've come and they wave they wave to all of
their friends back home and then they don't know why
but they start to cry

Sam and I leave the mall

We get home
She wants me to play with her ponies
Ponies all over the place
Pink ponies
We keep trying to wean her off them

"Don't you want to play with some planes Sam?"
We both try
Eric more than me
But no luck
Just as well
Don't know what we'd replace them with
They don't make drones in Fisher-Price
Not yet anyway
But give it time
Five years max

Eric gets home
He can tell me how his day was
Every detail free to share
He tells me about the guy who lost ten thousand bucks
and laughed his ass off
The couple who couldn't stop groping each other
under the table
The sad the desperate
Every detail every one

I myself have had a non-classified day for once
So I tell him about the mall
About the ponies
I don't have much to tell but it is a pleasure to tell it
I don't tell him about the cameras
The Indians

Tired all of a sudden
Hits me like G-LOC
I sleep the rest of the week
Must need to catch up
Snooze button for a while then turn it off altogether
Not peaceful sleep though
Guilty
I know Sam's waiting wants her special time but I need
to sleep

I wake up with ponies on my pillow
Surrounding me
Pink ponies everywhere
Guess we had special time after all

Week's too fast
Too fast and I'm back on the road driving downrange
to my twelve hour ahead world
Driving into a sunrise that's a sunset

I tap the outgoing pilot and he gives me a look as I
take over the controls
I don't know what it's about until I sit down look at the
screen
He's been lingering
Lingering over the dying
A mound of the dying
Our dying
The medics are miles away and I am to orbit over the
dying bodies
Linger
With no idea of who they are or how they got here
Linger
As their thermal readings cool
Change
As one by one their bodies slowly turn the same grey
as the sand
Linger
As one by one they
A mound of our grey
Our boys in grey

Please
Let me find the guilty who did this the military age
males who did this send me to shred their bodies into
pieces too fine for my resolution

But my orders are to linger

Linger
It's a long day

Hard to go home tonight
The desert isn't long enough
Still have bodies in my head
I orbit our block a few times
Hope Eric isn't looking out the window
Then I pull up and the door opens and the happy
family greets their hero home from the war
Every day
Every day
Every day they greet me home from the war

It would be a different book
The Odyssey
If Odysseus came home every day
Every single day
A very different book

We're having dinner and Eric waves his hand in front
of my face says,
"Hey.
Hello?
Honey?
You gotta clap off the game"

I say clap off the what?

He says, "Clap off the game. Blackjack. The end of my
shift.

*(He performs a blackjack dealer "nothing up my sleeves"
move with his hands to the eye in the sky.)*

(of the eye in the sky) To let it know I've got no chips up
my sleeve. But it's for me too. I clap and I'm done. I
leave the table and I'm done for the day"

I say good for you

He says, "You should make up your own. A dealer
makes up his own"

I tell him to shut the fuck up
But I do try it I do
Next day
After a day of grey

(She does, trying to find a signature move, a gesture that will bring relief, change something. Her gesture may involve some attempted wiping clean of the eyes. Nothing changes.)

But it doesn't

I sit in the driveway
Doing it in the driveway
But it doesn't

I can't go in yet
I don't know why
I imagine them
Inside
I try to see them
Close my eyes
Get a thermal reading

Sam is in her bed

Eric's on our couch

I am in the car

...

New mission today
Big one
No jeeps
No IEDs
No dead grey mounds
A real mission
A personality strike
We're on the hunt
The hunt for Number Two

The Number Two

We are to find him and we are to eliminate him
But we are to take our time
The headset stresses certainty
Target certainty is key
There have been mistakes
It has to be him
Number Two
Not his uncle not his brother not his gardener not his
chef
Him
Make sure it is him

Will do
The man's as good as dead
We will smite him down

I tap the previous god out take the controls
Observe the convoy below
This is the Number Two convoy
One of these vehicles is the Number Two

My knuckles are white as I stare down
The convoy stops in the middle of nowhere
A man gets out
Zoom
A woman
Oh well

The convoy splits up
Shit
Which do I – ?
Headset
I follow the car they tell me to follow
The guiltiest-looking one
Not the flashiest car but it's fast
Looks kinda like mine
Actually

Is that – ?

No

I think it is

Weird

My car sure likes to drive in the desert

Same war different desert

Or same desert different war

No different desert different war

I don't know

Anyway

That's fuckin' weird

I follow the car that looks like my car until I am tapped out

(She tries out a move. Nothing.)

It doesn't

I drive home

I see myself from above as I drive what I would look like

A tiny grey car driving through a grey desert

Tiny and grey and guilty

Huh

I can't breathe

I need some air

Even if it's desert air I need air

I stop the car

Half stop half crash whatever

Discover you can do that

Stop in the desert

It's not just a space to cross

It can be a place to stop

I turn off the car

Feel things settle

Quiet

I get out

Breathe the heat
Feel my heart slow
I stare up at the black
Remember the blue
And then I walk
I don't know why but I walk through the sand keep
walking am compelled to walk like those Indians
through JC Penney as something pulls me up and over
a ridge and there I find them
Crosses
Hundreds of crosses hammered into the sand
No names just crosses
Somebody put them here
Maybe on the way home
As some kind of
Bringing it out of the grey
Making it real

I go back to the car
I grab all the garbage on the floor and bring it back
with me and stick it in the sand
Some cold fries for the IEDs
A burger wrapper for the jeep
A bottle of backwash Pepsi for our grey boys
I add them to the field
I wait for something to happen

*(She waits. She tries another motion, perhaps looking to
the sky, the heavens. Nothing.)*

But nothing

Eric was worried I was late sees the sand all over the
car
I don't want to talk about it I go into Sam's
She's deep asleep in her big girl bed
I kiss her forehead
I stare at her

She's grey
She's grey she's grey she's grey
I grab her is she not breathing is she why is she grey
why
Why

She screams awake
Eric turns on the light
Color comes back
She's pink again
Pink is good pink is very good I'll take pink now I'll
take it

Eric looks at me a little funny
I tell him to cut it out
He says come watch the screen
Our favorite show is on
I say not mine
I go to our bedroom
To be alone
To slccp
If I could just sleep
Eric comes in instead
Eric wants to talk
I don't
Eric says counseling
He read on the website there's Air Force counseling
Office right here in town
He wants to go tomorrow
I tell him I'm tired
I'm so
But fine whatever fine

So I wake up, drop special Sam off, cross the desert,
follow Number Two or the alleged Number Two,
we all know he's Number Two but we need to know
know and he hasn't let us know yet, leave the grey,

cross the desert and hit a couch with Eric in front
of a blonde with glasses who asks us questions, Eric
probably has a hard-on for her, this brainy piece of
civilian tail, maybe he's getting ideas, trade me in
for a babe with less baggage, but fine, I'll be a good
sport, I'll stay, I'll listen to Blondie's questions, I can't
answer half of them, security clearance, not in front
of them I can't, and you know, I don't really want to
talk about anything anyway because if I was in a war,
a real war, we wouldn't be having this conversation, I
wouldn't be fucking exhausted, my head full of grey
sitting on a couch talking to an Air Force – approved
shrink with my husband, no, I would be having a beer
with my boys, I would be shooting pool, I would be
cranking music, I would not not not be sitting on a
couch talking about my feelings our relationship what
our relationship is what we want it to be I would not
so can we pretend can we do that can we pretend that
I don't come home every night every single fucking
night can we do that can we do that very simple thing
can we can we can we all pretend that I'm really in a
real fucking war

The shrink asks me a question
Like I'm the guilty
I want to tell her
You don't know guilty
I know the guilty
I see the guilty every day
Don't speak to me of guilt
Don't speak to a god of guilt
This god isn't interested okay?
This god wants a beer

I tell Eric we're not going back
He's upset
Poor guy must've really liked that blonde

Eric tells me to at least take off the flight suit to please

take it off before I come home
I tell him no
It's how I know
It's how I know who I am

Back to Number Two
He just drives
Drives around in my car
I think he knows we're there
We're miles above him but I think he knows
So he doesn't get out
If he got out we'd have target certainty and it would
be over
So he drives instead
Or is driven
The eternal passenger
But he has to get out sometime
To piss or something
Right?
How does he piss?
Into a cup or something?
Number Two is the one who calls himself a prophet
Perhaps prophets don't piss
I trail the non-pissing prophet
Trail him through his grey desert
Twelve hours a day
White knuckles the whole way
Just like his
You can't tell me his knuckles aren't white
Knowing I am above him Death is above him
Waiting
Waiting
Waiting for that one mistake
Oh his knuckles are white
You can't tell me they're not

I stop at the crosses
Put a few more Pepsis into the sand
I forgot some squirters from a few weeks back
Left some unaccounted for
My own section now my own plot
Drive home
I am above me I am me
I'm not entirely sure where I am

Sam wakes up during dinner Sam wants to play with her ponies
Those fucking ponies
I pick her up
Are you a hair-tosser after all Sam? Are you a hair-tosser?
Sam's confused
Eric takes her from me
Fine
But she should remember
She should remember the sky

Eric and I lie side by side
No sex for a while
Sex takes me to another place and I don't need another place right now I have about all I can handle
More
Don't think Eric minds
He seems somewhere else too

My alarm goes off and I spot something gold on the nightstand
Eric left me a present
A square wrapped in paper from work
Paper from the Pyramid
Pyramid paper
A Post-it on it his writing
"For the drive home"

Cryptic

My husband's getting cryptic
I toss it in the passenger seat

I'm late
My seat-warmer is pissed when I tap him out says,
"Don't ever do that again I have to get home in time to
get my kid to –"
I say fine
I take the controls
I follow the Prophet

Will I be the one?
Will it be my shift?
So much time invested in this in you
I don't want to come into work one morning and find
you're gone
That my seat-warmer got you
That you are no longer in the grey
It has to be me

I arm myself with coffee
Cup after cup
I watch his car my car
Nine hours
Doesn't he need gas?
Maybe he's like me
Never stop never land

I know he's in there
Wishing he could call someone
Ask for help
But he can't
He picks up the phone we'll have him
So he prays to himself instead
White-knuckled
Prayers
Or prophecies
Prophecies no one will hear

Prophecies that end at his windshield

Wait

The car stops

Shit

The driver door opens and a man walks out

Could it – ?

Zoom

No

No limp

Our man has a limp

And is missing an eye of course they're all missing eyes for some reason

You can't be a Number Two unless you're missing one

No

This is not my man must be his driver

Zoom

What's that in his hand?

A rifle?

A gun?

No

Just a

Bottle?

Maybe?

A bottle it looks like a

I think it's a Pepsi

Huh

He tosses something out of the Pepsi

Pepsi?

No

Piss

It has to be piss

Prophet piss

You fucker

You fraud

You fucker I know your game I know you I got you now

But then the piss makes me want to go
Fucker
I still have another half-hour
It's not a fair fight if one of us has to go
But I am going to kill you screaming bladder or not
and there is absolutely nothing you can do

I hold it
Hold it
I'm tapped out
Fuck
Fine tomorrow then
Fine

I drive through the static
Stop and stick a bottle in the sand
A promise an IOU
Piss in it for good measure

Get back in the car
Try to breathe
See the gold on the seat
Eric's present
I unwrap the Pyramid
It's a CD
Jesus
One of Eric's mix CD's
Permanent marker on it:

"Decompression"

What the fuck?
I slide it in

*(We hear the CD mix in a sonic collage – it begins with
AC/DC and ends with "The Pony Song":)*

PONY SONG

WHERE O WHERE WILL WE RIDE TODAY

O THE PLACES WE'LL SEE
WHERE O WHERE WILL WE RIDE TODAY
MY PRETTY PONY AND ME

(**THE PILOT** *smiles, she has been given some relief.*)

THE PILOT.

Eric
He's still got it
And it's perfect timing
The pony ride ends just as I pull into our drive
Home
I'm Home
Home

I kiss him when I walk in
The second I walk in
He says, "You liked it?"
I loved it and I tell him so

A flicker of sadness as he sees I still have the suit on
but I ask him if he wants to take it off if my husband
who I love wants to take it off
He does but there's Sam she's awake she had a bad
dream and she needs a story first
I read to her to my little girl to my angel
She's a little grey as I walk out of her room but it's a
trick of the light the dark

Eric opens me up
Every zipper every one
He tells me I'm brave
He tells me he loves me
He tells me he wants me
I pull him to the floor
I see us from above
Our heat overloading the sensors
Shorting them out
His face

His face is a bit blurry
I turn on a light
Better
I come back to him
He touches me
I grab him
I make him move left
Right
No 1.2 second delay
I slide him in
He's ready to go
I'm ready too but don't want to be don't want to let go
of where I am who I am this feels good enough and I
don't want to push it don't want to go somewhere else
want to stay here in this this
He goes and I fake it

We breathe together on the floor
His face
He's so happy
So happy
He thinks he's solved something
Oh Eric

We get into bed
He cuddles in
He's gone
I stare at the ceiling
See shapes there
Shadows to decipher interpret destroy
I close my eyes
I see us from above
I pull back
I see our home
Back
Our block

Back
Our city
Back
Our
All of it
I see it all

Open my eyes
I'm naked
Cold
I slip on my suit and get back into bed

Sun too soon
Eric
Eric's still here
Looking at me
Heartbroken
The suit

He showers
I don't bother
I'm already dressed
We don't talk at breakfast
I take his hand
I squeeze it
He has to know
It's him
Him and Sam
They are my true corn

Sam enters on cue and I hold her so tight so tight
She groans and pushes me away
She has a pony in her hand
"Look Mom," she says and I do
"I can make her fly"
And she flies that pony all over the room that fucking
pony flies that pink pony soars

Eric is crying and I wish I could wish I knew this was a
real moment wish I knew this was where I am
But wherever I am I love it it makes my heart soar
I'll carry that I'll try to carry that into the grey

I kiss them goodbye
Something's going to happen so I kiss them goodbye
Sam makes me kiss her Pegasus too
I do it
Gladly
I take them in
Eric
Sam
Me with my belly on the wall
And I'm gone

…

The desert again the Pyramid disappears and I put in
"Decompression"

(The music plays.)

Not how it was intended to be heard but it seems right
Backwards seems right

I pass the crosses
No time for them now
Chuck some shit out the window anyway
My pin and some other shit
They'll drift over one day
Find their home

I wait in my parking spot for the CD to finish

("The Pony Song" concludes, **THE PILOT** *singing along
to the last line:)*

MY PRETTY PONY AND ME

And I step out

"You stink," my 19 year–old says

Thanks
I face the screen
The desert
The war
I follow the Prophet
I follow his car my car
It will be today
I know it will be today
I will be the one
I will be the one to erase you
You are the Prophet but I am God
And you do not speak for me

Eleven hours nothing
Patience
Patience
Then
My car leaves the desert
It comes to a village

It stops in front of a home a humble home
The headset gets excited this is his home this is where
he keeps one of his wives one of his families this might
be something

I wait
White-knuckled
But my car just idles
Sits there idling
No one on the team understands what's happening
Why is the car just sitting there sitting there outside his
home?

They don't understand
I understand
God understands

He's just looking
Looking out the window

At them they must be there in their window
He wanted to see them that's all
One last time
Wanted to see the ones he loved

Get out
Out
Out you coward
Out

Fuck
The car pulls away
It's over
Over
My last chance
Wait
The edge of the screen
A woman
No
A girl
A girl runs out of the house
Runs out toward the car
A little girl running
Her face her body blurs
And
Miracle
The car stops
The passenger door opens

The Prophet
The one-eyed Prophet walks out
Leaps out
Leaps limping toward her waving his arms
He's waving her away waving her away from the car
trying to keep her safe

The headset shrieks
"It's him it's him

Sights sights"
My 19 year-old locks the laser crosshairs dead on
He locks on and I wait for the call to push my button
To send the Prophet to Hell
"Take the shot
Take it"
I will
For God is mightier than her Prophet
In 1.2 seconds God is going to call her Prophet home

But then
The girl
Her face
She stops running and I see it
Her face
I see it clearly
I can see her

It's Sam
It's not his daughter it's mine
It's Sam
She has Pegasus in her hand she wanted to show him
Pegasus

The team screams fire and all it would take is my
thumb my thumb has orders to annihilate but it's her
it's her and I can't kill her I can't kill her I can't

I know in a moment someone will push me aside
someone will push the button for me the team will
correct me ·
And I know I can't let that happen

The screen
I have to get Sam off the screen
I don't control the camera the camera is on Sam
I don't control the camera
But I control the plane

I pull back on the throttle with both hands
In 1.2 seconds I see the screen lurch blur
I pull the Reaper's snout up up
Higher higher
Belly up
I turn its Gorgon eyes to the sky
Turn its swollen belly to the sky
Do not stare at Sam
Stare at the sky instead
The innocent sky
Stare at this you fucker stare

(We see blue.)

And it's there
It's there
It's there in the grey
It's there
I see it

(Blue disappears.)

Then black
The screen goes black
Eleven million dollars of black

The headset but I am not it anymore I am not the team I am alone again the lone wolf and I have saved my daughter
I let the headset fall to the ground
I turn
Expecting to see all eyes on me

But they are not
The eyes are on the screen instead
The screen
Sam is back on the screen
Why is she back on the screen

My Commander
My Commander is here he smiles a sorry smile says
"We had our eye on you Major
For weeks
The warning signs
Everything is Witnessed"

Oh
Oh
That's why she's still
There was another one
There was another Reaper above me I didn't know
there was another god above me but there was

Another pilot another trailer
Sam
I leap out of my seat but am held back
My 19 year-old holds me back
Somewhere the button is pushed

I scream at the screen
I watch
I watch the Prophet
I watch him look at the sky the approaching Hellfire
Sam please Sam Sam Sam
He hears me he does the Prophet he grabs her and
he pulls her to him covers her eyes with his embrace
shields her tiny body as best he can cradles her in his
arms so tight so tight so tight
Thank you
Thank you
Shukran
Shukran

The team cheers as my daughter dies
As her arms and legs fly off in separate directions
As her pulp is mixed with the car and the Prophet and
the sand

As her pulp dissolves into the grey
There is only the grey now
Only the grey

…

*(Lights shift. A moment. The Pilot achieves a state
of peace, of power. The sound of static grows over the
following, starting imperceptibly.)*

It is grey here
But it is concrete not sand
It does not shift
This is my home now
My court–martial home
I am here
Grounded

They must have taken my suit
But I still see it it is still here
I earned it
I earned it through sweat and brains and guts
Guts they will never understand
Guts *you* will never understand

*(She takes in the audience, addresses them even more
directly than before.)*

You
You who watch me
Who observe me watch my every move here and I know
you watch me I know there is a camera somewhere for
Everything is Witnessed
You who have slaughtered my child
Sealed me in this tomb
Away from my husband
My blue
You who seal me in a tomb and think you are safe
Know this

Know That You are Not Safe
Know That You Can Keep Me Here Forever You Can
Bury Me in a Bunker of Grey But That Does Not Protect
You for One Day it Will Be Your Turn Your Child's Turn
and Yea Though You Mark Each and Every Door with
Blood None of the Guilty Will Be Spared
None

None

None

(She successfully performs her motion.)

boom

(Sound and lights out.)

End of Play